IF SHE'S FREE, I AM FREE

IF SHE'S FREE, I AM FREE

JEREMIAH HASLAM

WE ARE UNRELENTING BOOKS

~ 1 ~

DEDICATED TO

THANK YOU

INTRODUCTION

CONTENTS
Chapter 1: **SUNDAY DINNER**
CHAPTER 2: **HOW IT ONCE WAS**
CHAPTER 3: **MEETING THE SHE-WOLF**
CHAPTER 4: **NOT MY CHILD**
CHAPTER 5: **THE UNTHINKABLE AND A DREAM**
CHAPTER 5: **RESISTANCE AND A BAD DREAM**
CHAPTER 6: **FREE**

~ 2 ~

DEDICATED TO

To the memory of our past ancestors who died in the struggle,
We have not forgotten you. May you live on in our memories,
as we remember our history and move into our future.

$$\sim 3 \sim$$

THANK YOU

To my lord and savior Jesus Christ for enable me to write, without you there would be no me. To my beautiful wife, Vanessa, you have been by my side every step of the way, love you always. To my beautiful daughter Rheanne, I 'am so proud of you, there is greatness in you. In time you will share the greatness in you with the world, Love you daddy's little girl.

~ 4 ~

INTRODUCTION

Not long-ago slavery was normal in the United States of Amer-
ican, because of the Degradation of the African man and woman
millions of lives were affected, physically, Mentally, emotionally.
The horrors of slavery and how African Americans were treated,
had a profound effect on me through the stories that I learned
about over the years. As an author I wrote this book as a reminder
of these events of the past that took place. May the world learn
from the failures of the past.

~ 5 ~

Chapter 1: SUNDAY DINNER

It was Mother's Day; my family and I attended church service and had a good time. The choir did not just sing but sang today. The sermon that the pastor preached profoundly touched my heart. The subject was, you meant it for evil, but God meant it for good, coming from the book of Genesis, chapter fifty, verse twenty, the sermon reminded me of where my family came from and how far the Lord has brought us from. My name is Hope; I am 90 years old, and the Lord has blessed me with good health. I can walk, talk, see, and hear. The Lord has been good to me. I have grandchildren, so I am known as Grandma Hope. As we came into the house and gathered around the dining room table to eat all that good cooking, my son Zion said a prayer over the food; we all then started to eat. After dinner, for dessert, we had my favorite good old sweet potato pie. Zion, his wife Victoria, and their three children, Lester Denial and his twin sister Hope, named after me, all came and sat in the living room together. My dog Goodnight came and sat by me so I could give him a treat; he was a 110-pound huskie German shepherd mix all black in color, loyal, and protective. I asked each of my grandchildren what they got out of the sermon. Hope was the first to respond and said she learned there is a purpose in everything in life, even when it's not good. I told them this sermon reminded me of where this family came from and how we made it to where we are today. Let me tell you about your great-grandparents. They were born into slavery, one of the most horrific things a human can be in, but they were fighters and determined. You all come from a line of courageous people. Remember, our people are strong, not weak. Let me tell you where this family came from.

CHAPTER 2: HOW IT ONCE WAS

Your great-grandparents, my mother and father, were born on a plantation in Florida; their names were Abraham and Abigail. Daddy was a tall, slim man who knew how to fix and build things. He only had one hand because the slave owner had cut it off. At 12 years old, Abraham tried to defend his father when the overseer started beating him for not picking cotton fast enough; Abraham jumped on the overseer, punched him, and told the slave owner don't hit my father. The master cut off his hand and told him, "Don't you ever raise your hand against a white man, Nig**." His mother cried and pleaded with the slave owner not to do it, but he did anyway; he did it out of hate and to teach the other slaves a lesson. Daddy survived but told his parents, "When I have a child someday, I pray their life will not be like this, that they will not be a slave but free." It was a dream that he would later be determined to see come to pass. Abigail, my mother, was a woman with dark, beautiful skin; she was a thin woman with a gift for working with plants and animals. Slave owners mistreated them and made them work from sunup to sundown in the fields picking cotton and tobacco, which brought slave owners money; as long the as slave owners were making money from the crops, the lives of slaves did not matter. But through it all, by the grace of God, many of them made it through those terrible times. As time passed, Abraham and Abigail fell in love and were married.

~ 7 ~

CHAPTER 3: MEETING THE SHE-WOLF

One day, as Momma walked outside the slave house, she noticed something black running around the chicken coop. As she walked closer to the pen, she noticed chicken feathers and blood on the ground, and something had killed one of the chickens. Sensing as if something was watching her, Momma turned around, and ten feet behind her was a black she-wolf. They both look intensely at each other, neither one making a move. The wolf was tall and had pretty black fur and gold eyes. Suddenly, a gunshot went off. Then, hearing a whimpering sound from behind the chicken coop, the she-wolf suddenly ran off into the woods. The slave owner came running up with the overseer and said, "I got him; he's a big one." They carried the animal's body from behind the shed. To Abigail's shock, it was a black wolf, like the one she had just seen but a larger male wolf. They asked her, "Have you seen any more wolves?" Usually, they run in packs. Abigail knew she could get in trouble for lying. Still, she felt terrible, for the she-wolf, her mate, was now dead, and she could have attacked Momma but did not. Quickly heading back to the slave house, Momma told Daddy about what had happened. He said, "You have a way with animals. They seem to like you. That's why she did not attack, and you meant her no harm." Momma said, "I hope they don't kill her." Thankfully, she got away.

CHAPTER 4: NOT MY CHILD

As the months followed, your great-grandmother became pregnant with me. Both parents were happy and sad at the same time because the life of a slave was not a good one, and they wanted their child to be free. I was born nine months later, and at that time, the slave owner started a new money-making venture selling gator skin. What was discovered was that many slave owners used the babies of slaves as bait for the alligators. The gator skin made much money, but a child's life for money was just plain horrific. The gator hunting was beginning to gain momentum, That was when the unthinkable happened. It did not take long for the slave owners to start using the babies of the slaves as bait. The slave owner and hunters took the infants for to be used as bait, If the parents resisted this horrific act, they were beaten, even killed, if they got in the way. Many mothers would scream a blood-curdling cry when their babies were taken for bait. Mother remembers one incident that shock her to the core, when the slaves were picking cotton; one of the new mothers, Ruth, had her three-month-old son on her hip. As she worked hour after hour, she was given time to nurse her infant. While the little one fed, mom and baby bonded. Mother looked over at Ruth, and then came the slaveowner, the

overseer, and his men. They called her, asking that baby finished feeding. The slaves had a bad feeling about this. Ruth said Yes, sir; all right he said, Give him to me, Ruth looked afraid as she gave him the baby the child wiggle as he was held upside down by one leg. One of the men said he would do well as bait; he's a lively little rascal. As they turned to walk away with the infant, Ruth said My baby as she tried to reach out to him. Both mom and child started crying; the young mother begged

and pleaded, but to avail; Hate and greed was showing its ugly head. She then ran in front of the men. The slave owner gave the order to get Ruth out of the way, she was knocked to the ground, falling on her face and whipped by the overseer. She sadly watched, murmuring the words he going to be hungry, he going to be hungry.

My parents had enough and were going to do whatever they could to make sure I was safe, even if it meant giving up their lives. Daddy and Momma came up with a plan. We heard stories of slaves escaping and heading north, so my parents decided to run away, but it would not be without opposition.

~ 9 ~

CHAPTER 5: RESISTANCE AND A BAD DREAM

Through the money that the slave owner was making, it was as if he knew we would try to escape, he would have the overseer do frequent checks on the babies to see how they were growing, and the repeated visits disturbed the chance for Mothers and Fathers to escape. There was one slave, Evan, who had to help catch Gator. He was deeply affected by the gator bait practice; he tried to escape but was caught and hung in front of all the slaves. The slave owner said he would not let anything get in his way of business and let this be a lesson to all his slaves who would try to escape. As the hunting went on, one night, Mother's worries and fears would hunt her dreams; as she slept, she appeared to be in the woods. She began to walk she could see the black she-wolf in the distance looking at her as Mother heard a baby cry and people talking in that direction; the she-wolf looked in that direction. She started running there, swiftly moving to the right and suddenly disappearing into the heavy part of the woods. Mother then heard the baby cry. As the cry got louder and louder, she heard Father say help her. As Mother ran in that direction, she saw a river and a man holding a baby over his head. As Mother got closer, the man turned and smiled; it was the overseer As he got ready to throw the baby in the water. Seeing that there were alligators in the water, Mother screamed "no, no, no. Then she woke up crying and telling Daddy Not my baby, not baby, she going be free. Daddy comforted her and said yes, she will be free.

~ 10 ~

CHAPTER 6: FREE

It was October 17, a day that is so important in our family history. As night fell hours after working on the plantation, Abraham and Abigail did not sleep but waited for the right time to make their escape. Suddenly, the slave owner walked through the door carrying a lantern and said, "Abraham, Abigail, I came to see the baby. It looks like she is growing well; we will be going gator-hunting. I think she will make good bait." Abigail looked at her husband and screamed, "No." The slave owner responded, "Don't be so emotional. Give me that baby! now." But Abraham jumped in the middle of them and said no; the slave owner then said, "Get out of the way," and pulled out his knife, but the years of abuse and mistreatment were no longer going to stop Abraham; he stood firm. "I told you to get out the way. You can make another baby nig***". But Abraham had made a club out of a tree branch and had it hidden in the shake and tied it to his waist. He had it hidden behind him; he pulled out the club and knocked the knife out of the slave owner's hand; the two then began to wrestle for an advantage. Abraham then told Abigail, "I won't. You and the baby know I love you both. Run, don't look back, be free. Abigail, with the baby in her arms, ran out of the shack. As the struggle between Abraham and the master continued, the lantern was knocked to the floor and fell on the straw bed, creating a fire that quickly engulfed the room; then quickly, the shack mother ran with me, holding on tightly with tears running down her face telling me we would make it; by the grace of God lord Jesus, we would make it. Heading to the woods, Mother entered the woods but began to hear the hunting dogs barking. If they caught up to her, she would be attacked viciously, and she and the child would die, but Mother kept going deeper into the woods. In the far distance behind her, she could see the fire. Thirty feet from her was the swamp and a boat by a dock with a torch to provide some light to the area. Mother's body was shaking, and her feet were bleeding from running barefoot in the woods, sticks. Had cut her feet. As she got closer to the boat, suddenly, a bullet hit her right in the leg. She quickly fell to the ground. Her foot fell into the water, and still holding me tight, crying and crawling away from the water, she then heard the voice of the master saying, "You think you were going to get away. Know you're going to pay, and you are going to wish! you were dead like Abraham." A dog was barking. It was Bruiser—a big, white and brindle descendant of the Molossus and the most vicious of the hunting dogs that killed many slaves—that came with the master. As the master got closer, he said, "This is the last time I will say this.Give me that baby I have this rope tight around my hand so this dog won't get ye but I, am ready to let him go." Mother turned over and moved away from the water, looking at her pursuer, bleeding, hurting, and exhausted, but a mother's love for her child would always remain strong. Mother mustered up the energy to utter the word "no." The master had a look of murder and evil intent in his eyes. Then, from the swamp came an alligator, grabbing Bruiser and taking down the master with it into the water because the rope was tightly around his hand both he and his dog were consumed by the gators. Mother, with everything she had left, shakingly crawled and grabbed the torch. Then she got into the boat, and using the row, she moved it down the swamp which connected to a large river. *As the boat moved slowly in the water, each foot brought us closer to my freedom and farther from slavery. The moon's reflection in the water caught my mother's eyes; she saw the black she-wolf with her pups standing at the riverbank, living free. She began to ponder on freedom, and at that moment, she uttered these words,* **"Though we were bound in chains and taken from our homeland by those that held power in their hands, the mind thought of being free. Though I was used, abused, and belittled by touch and words, my mind must be free. If the eagle is free, the wind is free, and if the wolf is free, God made them as He made me. The Creator of the heavens and the earth, the Lord God Almighty, made man in His own image; male and female, whether with black skin, white skin, or any other color, I have the right to be free. The majestic wolf—strong, intelligent, and beautiful, but an animal. If she's free, I am free."**

THE END

~ 11 ~

John **3:16** For God so loved the world that He gave His only begotten Son, that whoever believes in Him should not perish but have everlasting life.

9 798218 281113